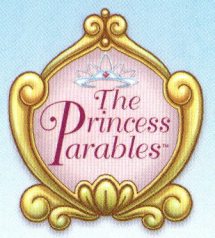

Princess Faith

Sticker & Activity Book

INSPIRED BY **Jeanna Young** & **Jacqueline Johnson**
ILLUSTRATED BY **Omar Aranda**

Once upon a time, in a magnificent castle near the sea, there lived five princesses.

Their names were
Joy, Grace, Faith, Hope, and Charity.

This is Princess Faith.

Find the stickers to finish the picture.

Princess Faith loves her bunny, Buttercup. Find some of Faith's other favorite things. Circle the words in the word search. Use the Word Bank.

```
K Z W D F T R C
G C Y A X E E E
U A I L T Z M B
J T R S A Q M U
H C I D D J U N
F S N D E A S N
K O O B G N E Y
C A S T L E V R
```

Word Bank

BUNNY   BOOK   FAITH   CASTLE
SUMMER   READ   SISTER   GARDEN

Faith loves to read.
Decorate the inside of these books.
Design your own covers.

This is Princess Faith's garden. Color all the flowers.

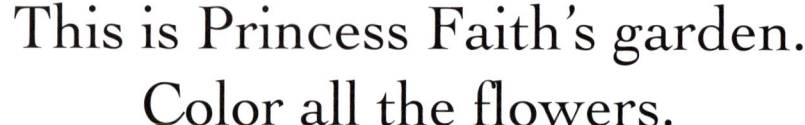

Help Princess Faith find Buttercup.

7

The princesses think the thunderstorm has destroyed their garden.

But then they see a single flower! Color Faith's garden.

Can you spot the differences between these two pictures? There are 6. Circle them.

The princesses are hard at work in the garden. Use the numbers to help color the picture.

1 = **yellow**   3 = **pink**   5 = **green**   7 = **red**

2 = **purple**   4 = **blue**   6 = **brown**

How many of each? Count the number of birds, butterflies, crowns, and flowers. Then write the number on the line.

HOW MANY?	NUMBER
(birds)	_____
(butterflies)	_____
(crowns)	_____
(flowers)	_____

Solve the secret code. Match a number with a letter and write it.

G	O	D		L	O	V	E	S		Y	O	U
7	15	4		12	15	22	5	19		25	15	21

22	5	16	25		13	21	3	8	!

A = 1   J = 10   S = 19
B = 2   K = 11   T = 20
C = 3   L = 12   U = 21
D = 4   M = 13   V = 22
E = 5   N = 14   W = 23
F = 6   O = 15   X = 24
G = 7   P = 16   Y = 25
H = 8   Q = 17   Z = 26
I = 9   R = 18

Finally all the flowers bloom in the garden. It looks beautiful!

Can you find the hidden items? Circle them.

Buttercup	2 books	bat	crow	garden shovel

Rosebud	Teddy bear

It is summer in Princess Faith's garden. But soon the season will change. These branches are from an apple tree. Draw what the branch will look like in each season.

SPRING

SUMMER

FALL

WINTER